I0822676

Faerie Boots

Beyond the Faerie Wall

Michelle Helen Fritz

CLEAR SPRING BOOKS LLC

MICHELLE HELEN FRITZ

FAERIE BOOTS

BEYOND THE FAERIE WALL

Faerie Boots by Michelle Helen Fritz

Boots Character Art: Jessica Walden

Chapter Heading Art: Michelle Helen Fritz

Cover Design: Wanderlust Ink & Tome LLC

Emerlyn Character Art: Samaiya Art

Formatting: E.A. Shanniak

Proofreading: Cathey N.

Published by Clear Spring Books LLC of Clear Spring, MD

Dedication

from Michelle Helen Fritz

Thank you so very much to my sister, Cathey! You are such a treasure.

Contents

Chapter One

In Search of Boots

Miss Emerlyn Adair glared at the towering Wall before her, suspecting beyond its stony facade and ivy-covered vines, her beloved feline companion awaited his rescue. She wasn't supposed to trespass, not beyond the erected barrier. Humans never had any luck with returning from the Faerie realm. But this was *Boots*! Her feline companion with the silkiest fur that she was gifted by her father on a dark evening in wintertide. Emerlyn had dutifully fed and cared for Boots, even though he could be a bit prickly and often fled from her cuddling like she was some ghoulish specter. Emerlyn couldn't just do *nothing* and *hope* for the best. She sighed as she shook out her empire-waisted dress and straightened her straw bonnet. She could do this!

Lifting one of her leather-booted feet, she placed the toe into a slight groove in The Wall and pulled herself up by her gloved hands. Repeating this action, she soon began to pant, and her hands grew damp beneath the leather gloves. Wispy curls clung to her clammy face and neck. With the pale moon shining its faint light down upon her, she reached the very top. Her chest heaved, her muscles aching as she fought to catch her breath. Emerlyn was too winded to do much but swing one leg over to the forbidden side, situating herself astride the massive fortification as her eyes scanned the new landscape before her. Her sapphire eyes widened as the glint of the golden leaves that topped the colossal mahogany trees swayed in the gentle breeze. Above the trees, the dusky horizon loomed large and imposing; a canvas of purples, blues, and pinks swirled together to embrace the twinkling teal stars. Why, even the moon shone brighter here with its beautiful turquoise glow.

No wonder humans who strayed to the other side never returned.

Emerlyn looked below to the ground. Fog wafted, rising and whirling, making it difficult to tell what lay under the mist. She blinked back the stars in her vision, listening to the thundering of her heart. Emerlyn's stomach dropped at the thought of the unknown before her. A shiver raced down her spine, settling in the marrow of her bones. Could she do this? If she didn't, then Boots would be lost forever. But if she did, if she went down into the fog, would she survive to see him and bring him home?

Boots was worth the effort, no matter how slick and foreboding the stony surface looked. His golden eyes appeared in her mind, entreating her to save him. With that thought, Emerlyn swung her leg over the wall to join the other. She pulled the violet hem of her dress to free it. Lowering herself, she clung to the top of the structure and tried to gain purchase with the toes of her boots. Emerlyn slipped and her legs dangled in the air as her heart began to hammer wildly. When she thought she could hang on no longer, her foot found a groove. Shifting her weight, she slowly descended the wall, finding more places to fit her hands and feet. The mist curled around Emerlyn, embracing her in a wispy hug, clouding her sight from everything beyond it. She drew in a shaky breath and closed her eyes. She could do this! Slowly, she exhaled and opened her hands to let go. She waited for impact, for surely it would come quickly, but instead, she landed gently on her feet.

Would she be home before Papa noticed her absence? The very last thing she desired was for him to fear for her or rail at her for her rash actions the moment she returned. When Emerlyn's body had ceased quaking enough for her to take a step, her ears caught the sound of a musical medley.

What is that, and where is it coming from?

Would that draw her cat's interest? Surely, the feline had plenty of opportunity to make his way very far into the land of faeries. Boots could be anywhere; he might not even be alive. Tears gathered in her eyes, and her bottom lip quivered. She didn't want to picture her ebony-colored pet that way. It was time to move!

Her feet began to carry her toward the musical notes as incandescent mushrooms, and the bright wings of insects lit her pathway through the forest and away from the oppressive fog. Brambles and roots seemed to reach up to block her way with menacing fingers reaching out to capture her, but Emerlyn continued onward being careful not to tread over any tiny creature.

Circular orbs of beaming teal light hung suspended in the ether, beckoning her to an opening in between the trees. Faerie lights, Emerlyn realized, as tingling pricked her scalp and made goosebumps form along her arms under her pelisse. She moved forward, scanning her surroundings until she was at the mouth of the glade. Violet and amethyst flowers rose up from the golden grass around her. Emerlyn's eyes widened as she spied a bonfire with minstrels playing lutes and mandolins around the rippling teal flames. Dancing couples dotted the scenery with their vibrant jewel-hued clothing, enthusiastic grins plastered upon their faces. Her eyes locked onto the delicately pointed ears and swishing tails some of the faeries possessed. Feathered and exquisite translucent wings arced from finely tailored greatcoats and cloaks, almost as if they had been carefully sewn onto the fabrics. Iridescent bubbles floated in the air, coasting along the breeze and enchanting her even more at the multi-hued lights that radiated from their glassy surface. While she had grown up hearing stories of these lands, mostly cautionary tales, she had never dreamed of what beauty they held.

Emerlyn's gaze snapped to a collection of tree stumps along one side of the glade as a raucous laugh filled the air. Her eyes narrowed, brows furrowing as she crept toward the area, trying to make out the beings in the shadowy depths. Nearest to her was a black cat. *Boots!* Emerlyn shoved her fist into her mouth, stifling the cry of joy that wanted to burst free. She didn't want to frighten Boots, and there was a chance the feline wasn't even him. She continued to tiptoe toward the group. There was an owl with large golden eyes and what looked like soft, downy brown feathers beside the cat. Across from the owl sat a fox with amber eyes and a shiny cinnamon-colored coat. A silver-hued raccoon with large, inky eyes caught sight of Emerlyn, and her heart skipped a beat. Regarding her quietly, the owl tilted its head to the side.

Beside the feline was a toad with lime-green stripes and squinty yellow eyes. Emerlyn shuddered when she caught sight of the amphibian. During her childhood, her cousin used to chase her with slimy frogs captured in his hands whenever he visited her family's estate. The tiny hairs along the backs of her arms rose on end. Bile crept up the back of her throat, and tears sprang to her eyes. Emerlyn's body stiffened, chilling her blood each time she heard a croak outside her bedchamber window at night.

Bringing herself back to the present, Emerlyn wondered if the animals gathered by the bonfire were in danger. Were they lured in by faeries who longed to feast upon their bones during this celebration? Her lungs seized as icy slush rushed through her veins. It was best to act quickly if that was the case. How many of the poor creatures could she save?

Reaching the gnarled stump with the feline resting atop it, Emerlyn hurriedly reached out for the cat. Picking it up, she clasped the beast to her chest, ignoring the startled meow that came from under her chin. The sudden longing to caress his fur with her fingers almost overtook her senses. The other animals were all watching Emerlyn now with looks of confusion and, dare she even say, amusement?

"Oh no, my nightmare continues on," droned a deeply masculine voice, causing her to jump and look behind her. But she could see no one there.

With her brows drawing together, Emerlyn gazed down at the cat. Golden eyes returned her stare before the feline shook its head. "You've no place here among us, *human*. If you don't release me this instant, I shall bite you as hard as I can. I've been very reasonable up to this point," the feline declared as his narrowing eyes filled with disdain.

Emerlyn couldn't speak; in fact, she couldn't move. All thoughts fled from her mind like a rushing river. When the cat brought his teeth toward her locked arms, she flinched and sucked in a breath. "Please don't," Emerlyn managed to squeak out.

"Release me!" the cat growled at her.

"But...," she stammered. "You look just like Boots. How is it that you are talking to me? I don't understand."

"*Boots*? What a ridiculous name! You've no great wit, I grant you that. Do you have any idea of the indignity such a name leaves one with? It's insufferable!" The feline's tail flicked back and forth with annoyance.

"I beg your pardon! I had no idea that you were... were..."

"A faerie?" he prompted, interrupting her. Emerlyn nodded down at him. Swallowing, she bent toward the stump and allowed Boots to climb from her arms. Emerlyn avoided the weary eyes of the other faeries in their Unseelie forms. Her face grew hot as she realized how foolish and absolutely ridiculous she must be to them as they silently judged her.

Leaping with grace, Boots settled, turning back to look up at her. "Be gone with you. I have no wish to *ever* endure your presence again."

"Do you think that I was so terrible to you after all the care I gave you?" Emerlyn asked, with hurt overshadowing her voice.

"Would you like to be kept like a pet? Held against your will? Forced to suffer the unwanted attention of another?" Boots replied, shuddering.

"No, I would not." Emerlyn's throat grew thick as her eyes grew misty.

Boots nodded, then he turned his back on her.

What was she to do? The haze that had led her to the glade had retreated. Her vision swam as panic squeezed her chest. How had she made it this far into Faerie? When Emerlyn tried to recall the path she had taken to reach the music, her mind blanked. Had she been lured, enchanted, by the music? Racking her brain for tidbits that she had gathered over her eighteen years, she couldn't recall obtaining the knowledge that music was harmful. Faerie food, drink, and, of course, a bargain were all recipes for doom, no matter if one was in Faerie or the mortal realm. But that wasn't right, was it? What about the story of the dancing princess whose feet grew bloody in her satin slippers as she danced herself to death? *Oh no.*

"You could risk a bargain with him, you do realize?" came a whispered voice next to her ear.

Emerlyn gasped. *Oh, my merciful Heavens!*

Her heart thundered wildly in her chest. Turning her head, Emerlyn came almost nose to body with a pixie who floated along the air before her. Ruby hair curled around the tiny faerie's pale face and hung down her back to rest between her white wings. Her dress looked as if it had been created from rose petals.

"A bargain? I don't dare risk it," Emerlyn murmured back.

"It wouldn't harm you if you enacted it correctly," the pixie said, tapping her index finger on her shimmering cheek. Her skin glistened as though thousands of crushed diamonds had been brushed along it.

"I just need to return home," Emerlyn replied, folding her arms across her body.

"You could, with help. *Bargain* with him."

"What could I possibly offer that he would want?" The idea that Emerlyn had anything to offer Boots was comical. What did a cat really need? Shelter? Not likely here in Faerie. Not food or drink either from the looks of the nearby feasting table. Of course, there was also the fact that he could shift into his Seelie form and manage very well with whatever task he needed to accomplish.

What does he look like in his other form? Is he tall? Would he tower over me? Is his hair just as dark and lucious as his fur? And what about his eyes? Would they still seem to stare into my soul with such piercing intensity when he gazes at me?

"Why are you still here?" demanded Boots in a voice that cut her almost as deeply as a dagger's sharpened tip. He was turned back toward her, glaring with unrepressed ire.

"I offer you a bargain." The words spilled past her lips as she tried to gather her wits. Emerlyn wanted to reach into the air and draw those words back into her body. This was a very bad idea!

"I decline," Boots spat back.

"Why?" the pixie asked as she flew toward the cat.

"I wholeheartedly don't like her. That's reason enough," he huffed.

Molten lava pooled in Emerlyn's blood as her skin heated. "How dare you!"

"How dare *I*?" Boots hissed back at her.

"Do you remember the state that you were given to me in? Nearly frozen to death and so weak I had to pour milk into your mouth? You were like that for days! And I never gave up on bringing you back to health. I saw a poor creature and only sought to help you." Emerlyn's eyes blazed with hurt and simmering anger as she gazed down at him.

"I didn't ask to be saved," he quietly replied.

"No, I suppose you didn't." Emerlyn hung her head, allowing a tear to escape and trail down her cheek. She always cried when she was frustrated, and that fact further enraged her. Her bones hurt, and her head weighed a ton. All she desired now was to be warm at home and in her bed, even if that meant she faced the night alone. Being on this side of The Wall all alone was a far worse fate.

"Nor did I ask for you to never allow me to leave the manor. You kept me in a cage, no matter that there were no bars to close me in, just windows and doors."

"Help me return home, and I shall never bother you again," she said, entreating him. After all, she was only in this predicament because of her worry for him.

"You can easily never bother me again. I shall simply take my leave," Boots replied, gaining his feet and pivoting away from her.

"*Please!*" she begged, the plea tasting like bitter ashes on her tongue. She hated to beg but had little choice in the matter. She was at his mercy, totally and completely. That one word seemed to halt him. Slowly, his head turned, and his eyes rose to hers, locking her into his fierce gaze.

The pixie next to her harshly inhaled. "Oh, we *never* say 'please' or even 'thank you' here. That's so *low,* so very *human.*"

Ignoring the little faerie, she spoke again. "Please help me. Take pity on a helpless human. I aided you in my realm; help me in yours. I know no other soul except for you."

Boots's teeth clacked together as he closed his eyes.

Emerlyn held her breath in anticipation to see what he would say or do next, the anger melting from her body like thawing snow.

"I want your word that you will never rescue another wounded animal and keep it locked away in your home to rot. Furthermore, I want your promise that you will *never* step foot into Faerie again. That once we are parted, you will never think of me again." Golden eyes peered unflinchingly into hers, assessing her, weighing and judging.

"You have my word, my promise," she said, exhaling. "Have we struck a bargain?" Emerlyn hated that a spark of hope lit in her heart. Perhaps he didn't find her so undeserving after all. Yet...faeries were such adept tricksters. Could she trust him?

Boots rolled his eyes, then jumped from the stump. The air shimmered as a burst of silver light exploded around him. In moments, the cat was gone, and in its place was a tall male faerie. The entrancing golden eyes and ebony hair that lay across his forehead were indeed strikingly similar to those of Boots. His mouth was luscious, and his nose was straight, adding a regal bearing to him. The faerie was elegantly dressed in a cobalt-blue greatcoat with a pristine white lace cravat peeking from its folds to frame his perfect features and fitted black trousers that displayed muscled thighs and legs. Gleaming dark boots graced his feet and calves. Boots was every inch the perfect rendering of an English gentleman, except for the pointed tips to his ears. Stars waltzed across her vision, and she had to remind herself to breathe again. He was the most gorgeous male Emerlyn had ever laid eyes upon, and the thought that Boots hated her tore a hole in her chest and shredded her heart in pieces at his feet.

Chapter Two

Faerie Forest

Alaric stood, looking down at Emerlyn, who, for once, was smaller than he. A tiny part of his heart relished that he was able to loom over the bonnet, which concealed the golden highlights of her chestnut tresses. This human had been his captor for nearly six months. It had been a great stroke of luck that the maid had left the sitting room window ajar just enough for him to sneak through. Freedom had never been more savory than when he had climbed The Wall and landed back into Faerie. It had been so long since he had shifted from one form to another that it hadn't been until just this moment that he had traded four legs for two.

"You require rest. Your legs will never carry you further tonight," he scoffed, his lips twisted into a sneer. "As for the bargain, listen well to me, *Emerlyn*. While I shall lead you to your home, you shall do as I previously stated; you will do as *I say* at all times."

"As you say? How can I vow to do such when you so obviously loathe me? You're a faerie, after all, and liable to trick me. Perchance you are twisting this bargain even now. I promise to follow you, but if for one moment I find myself in danger, my word is revoked," she rushed to interject.

"Remember, *human*, I am doing *you* the favor here. You would do well to heed my words. You can manage that, can't you?"

It was remarkable to watch the girl's face change colors so easily. She had grown an alarming shade of white, which, upon further consideration, might not be such a terrible thing if it were to kill her, absolving him completely from entering into any troublesome bargain with a *human*. Now, her face resembled a flaming tomato, and he knew to make this comparison since he had watched the fruits growing along a vine from the kitchen window of Emerlyn's home. He was aggravating her, and he was disturbed to discover that a teeny thought niggled in his mind, cautioning him against ill-treating her. *What in all the realms!* He hastily banished the thought from his mind.

"You should listen to *Boots*," croaked a toad that appeared next to the tree stump where her former companion had been seated.

Alaric looked to Emerlyn, her sapphire eyes blazing with tumultuous emotions, as she met his friend, Toadles, gaze.

"Oh, I suppose it's perfectly safe for me, a mere *human*, to trust you!" She looked around at the group who were all still and silent in their appraising contempt of the invading human. "You help me, then I go away. How difficult could that possibly be?"

"For me, it's near torturous. But I suppose 'tis the only way to get you permanently out of my life," Alaric sighed defeatedly. "We have an accord."

Emerlyn lifted her chin and narrowed her blue eyes, she was clearly rankled. "Shall we shake hands to seal the bargain?"

Alaric's lip curled. "What kind of monster are you? There's no handshaking here nor are there any words of gratitude. A verbal agreement does quite nicely."

"What kind of monster am I? I should say the same of you!" she scoffed as her eyes shone with inner fire.

He couldn't stop his eyes from rolling before he icily replied, "The niceties that exist in your *world* are frowned upon *here*. We *faeries* don't conduct ourselves to *your* staid societal rules. *You* would do well to conform to your current setting."

He watched her face mottle between embarrassment and anger, finding himself quite tickled knowing he so easily angered her. Alaric took a step closer, staring down his nose at her just to see what the slight little woman would do. Emerlyn closed the final space between them, rising up on her toes and glared fiercely.

"Ready when you are," she challenged, eyes gloriously ablaze.

Alaric's lips curled upward. "As I've said, you're much too tired to travel further tonight, so sit here and be quiet. You might even learn something valuable."

Emerlyn gathered her skirts in her hands and angrily stomped past him to the log. She took a seat upon the very end. Alaric grinned, preening inside about extorting her flammable temper. He strode over to her and knelt down onto the damp grass, inwardly flinching that he was soiling the knees of his trousers. As it couldn't be helped, he got down to the business of their bargain.

"Emerlyn, be a *good girl* and I shall see you safely returned home." He brought a fingertip to her satiny lips, hushing her words. Her eyes widened with indignation at his touch and possibly at his command, but he continued on. "You *will* listen to me; you don't realize the trouble these lands could present to you. Do nothing unless I say, and for the realms sake, don't attempt to rescue anyone or anything. Remember this: every creature will seek to devour you, to trick you, no matter how benign they may seem. You can't trust a single being here."

Leaning away from his finger, Emerlyn perked a brow at him. "Most especially you."

"Sweetling," Alaric lowered his voice, and he bent forward, invading the space she had created between them, "*especially* me. But as this is a bargain and faeries can't lie, you have my vow that I shall not harm you nor allow another to."

Searching her eyes as he spoke, Alaric found himself drowning in their depths. A muscle in his jaw ticked at the discovery that he was enamored of her. Here was a human who was dangerous to him. The only way to determine just how dangerous she might be to him was to taste her lips, and that, he would never do. He would see her safely home and then wash his hands of her once and for all. His well-being depended upon it. Humans were so fragile, so frail, so...

"I accept your terms," Emerlyn said, bristling, then straightened her shoulders. She was glorious in her determination to leave her vexation simmering beneath her skin.

They wouldn't get far tonight, no matter how much he pushed her. The desire to be rid of the girl meant nothing compared to the almost certainty that setting out now would only lead her to a clumsy injury. Then he'd have to suffer her presence for far longer than he could stand. Looking away, his eyes came to rest on Seline, the pixie that had broached the idea of the accord. Alaric's eyes narrowed to slits as she met his gaze and folded her arms across her chest.

"What?" Seline seethed, baring her pointy teeth.

"Would you mind taking Emerlyn to my tent and keeping an eye on her until dawn?"

"Why me?" Seline huffed incredulously.

"As this was your idea that I help her, you can now do your part." Alaric curved his lips into a grin, the dimple on his right cheek appearing.

"Oh, very well, come along, human. I was growing quite bored anyway. This lot can be so tedious." Seline flew toward Emerlyn and hovered in the air before her.

Emerlyn rose from the log, scanning the group, her movements graceful. She nodded to Seline and took two steps after the flying pixie before she halted, canting her head to look back at him. "I realize that I can't very well call you Boots. What shall I address you by?"

Holding her gaze, Alaric spoke. "'Boots' will do. There is no need of you ever knowing my true name, nor having a reason to use it."

Emerlyn's brows furrowed as she replied, "But you do so despise the name. I don't wish to anger you every time I need to call you something."

"Call me whatever you like. Whether 'tis Boots or some other foolhardy name. I care not." Alaric allowed his eyes to stay hard, like imposing marble, as he regarded her. Emerlyn said nothing more to him as her lips pressed tightly together. Turning, she kept her head held high as she followed Seline into the shadows of the evening.

It was mid-morning, and Emerlyn was limping. Alaric suspected her boots weren't well-worn, and now she bore a blister or two.

Whether the blisters were created last evening or were new today, he didn't know and most certainly *didn't care.* There was nothing he would do about an injury anyway. The insufferable human brought this fate upon herself, leaving the safety of her realm to traverse the wilds of Faerie in the dogged pursuit of her plaything as if he could ever belong to the likes of a mere mortal. This entire situation rankled him to no end. Alaric's nose wrinkled with disgust.

The rose-gold sun warmed them with its soft rays as it peeked through the thick foliage of the forest. Alaric swatted away an incessant insect with his hand as he peered back at her. Emerlyn was watching the ground, taking care with each step she made, though the scowl upon her face told him that she was still annoyed. A gurgle sounded from behind him, and he whirled around to see what creature was about to attack. Lifting his hand toward Emerlyn, he stayed her progress. The intensity of his gaze relaxed after a few moments when nothing pounced upon them.

"Let's—" he began, lowering his hand.

Another growl rent the ether, and his eyes rounded as they traced a path through the air to the human's stomach. Emerlyn brought both of her hands to rest against the offensive sound.

"Did you not eat?" he asked her. He already knew the answer. He'd heard her stomach grumble from where he was. But would the human tell him the truth or lie?

"Not much, no. I don't see much sense in eating Faerie food that will just entrap me forever here in these lands."

Alaric snorted. "All that you have been given was expressly with the purpose of ensuring your success in returning to the Mortal Realm."

"Anyway, that was hours ago, and we have not stopped once." Emerlyn shrugged her delicate shoulders, completely bypassing his comment. Rolling his eyes and pinching the bridge of his nose, Alaric exhaled.

"This is going to take an age."

"I am sorry—"

Holding up his index finger, Alaric interrupted, "We never apologize."

"Here in Faerie, yes, I suppose that is so, Bumblebee." She smirked at him, fanning her long, thick, dark lashes at him.

"*Bumblebee*?" he jeered.

"You *did* say to call you whatever I liked. That happened to come to my mind at that moment."

Rolling his eyes, Alaric turned away from her and set about again. He heard the rustling of her dress's muslin material and the soft press of her boots into the foliage beneath them. He trudged a path forward until they came to a separation of trees. His ears picked up the tinkling of a waterfall, and Alaric knew he would stop for his human.

His human?

Emerlyn wasn't his anything unless you counted what a huge pain in the backside she was, and he really should count that so he didn't forget the fact again.

Venturing further into the clearing, Alaric kept a steady pace. They walked in silence except for the occasional gurgle of the girl's stomach. The golden blades of grass were higher in the meadow. Lilac-colored bees flitted from one robin's-egg-blue wildflower to another. The waterfall grew louder. When they were a short distance away from the bubbling edges of the amethyst water, Alaric slid down to his knees, lowering a wooden basket from the crook of his elbow to rest beside him. Raising his eyes, he quirked his eyebrows at Emerlyn, silently instructing her to sit and rest.

When she was dutifully seated beside him, Alaric lifted the basket's lid and peered inside. Rifling through its contents, he chose a hunk of cheese and a packet of crackers. Withdrawing them, he set them onto his lap and again reached inside the hamper. His fingers found the silver-handled dagger, and he revealed it with a flourish, twirling it in the air. Settling the blade on top of the basket, Alaric began unwrapping the fare. He sliced the cheese and set each piece onto a square cracker. His attention was drawn to Emerlyn as she reached up to untie the lilac ribbons of her bonnet, drew it from her head, and set it down next to her. Her upswept hair was gathered into a bun at the nape of her neck and held with pearl-tipped pins. Alaric hurriedly aimed his attention back to his task. It wasn't a feast by any means, but when he handed it over to his traveling companion, she smiled at it brightly as if he held a five-course dinner in his hands for her.

A tingle grew in his belly as Alaric looked at her. Warmth crept over his skin and flowed into his heart. He wanted to reach out and capture Emerlyn's cheek in his palm, just to feel how soft her smile felt beneath his fingers. It was ridiculous. The worst idea that had ever popped into his head. Alaric scowled. No, this was not right. She was a *human*, after all. Whispering under his breath, Alaric gathered the contents of the basket and practically threw the food at her in his haste to be done with this task. He watched as she fumbled with her meal, and the beautiful smile that he *liked* slipped away.

Alaric steeled his heart to not feel a thing. Not one iota of anything *soft.* He pushed to his feet and clasped his hands together behind his back before he walked off and paced the meadow. Emerlyn remained silent in his wake. His thoughts were in turmoil, and he didn't know how to make sense of the emotions his heart was feeling. In the Mortal Realm, all he longed for was Faerie and his freedom. The two were synonymous. Weren't they?

His ruminations were brought to an astonishing halt when a high-pitched wail tore the atmosphere into pieces around him. Alaric felt something grip onto his ankle, piercing through the leather of his boot, pricking his skin. Before he could take stock of the situation, he was being dragged across the grass toward the pool of water. He tried to kick out with his free foot, but he couldn't find a being to strike. His fingers clung at the grass, trying to slow his progression, but failed as Alaric plunged into the frigid liquid, knocking the air from his lungs. His ebony hair floated above his head as he attempted to locate his assailant. His fist met firm flesh, but his actions lacked force as the water slowed his hand and lessened the brunt of his impact. Twisting around, Alaric saw beady black eyes and savagely tipped teeth much too close to his face. Had he still possessed air, he might have screamed in terror.

Chapter Three

The Terror of the Falls

From her spot upon the grass, Emerlyn's eyes widened as she sat frozen with shock and fear. The bite of cracker and cheese fell from her open mouth, landing on her lap. Her guide was being taken hostage, and there wasn't a single thing she could do but watch him drown and be eaten—hopefully dead before the crunching of his bones reverberated in her ears. Emerlyn's stomach churned, and bile rose to her throat. She willed the contents back down as her eyes watered.

Boots hadn't even yelled as he'd slipped under the water's hauntingly beautiful surface, here one moment and gone the next. What was she to do? She wouldn't just sit idly by; she couldn't! No matter that Boots hated her and wanted nothing more than to be rid of her. She couldn't fathom this as being their goodbye. She might be in Faerie amongst horrible creatures, but she wasn't one. She'd never meant to keep Boots captive. If only there was a way to prove her worth to him, and she couldn't do that if he died.

Pushing the food from her lap, Emerlyn crawled on her belly toward the water. Before she reached the lip of the rocky edge, Boots crested the surface and was spluttering, taking in huge gulps of air. Their gazes locked, both sets of eyes wild with terror.

Emerlyn tried to reach for him, but before her hands could grasp onto his sodden clothing, he disappeared back underwater. She hissed with annoyance; she had been so close! Her eyes intently stayed locked onto the pulsing water, waiting for another chance to grab a firmer hold.

Boots's head rose above the foam as his golden eyes furiously blinked the moisture from them. Emerlyn stretched her arms further toward him and felt his wet greatcoat slip between her fingers. She attempted to grab the material again, but her fingers wouldn't close around it. Her brows crashed together in puzzlement.

"Feel free to help me at any time!" Boots bellowed.

"I am trying! I simply...I can't!"

Boots ground his teeth together and said, "Emerlyn, I beseech you to aid me! Listen to my request and find some sharp instrument to give me." Then, he once again was being taken from her.

It was as if a huge weight was lifted from her shoulders the moment he spoke the words. A rush of relief flowed through her body, freeing her limbs to do as she desired, not to be bound up in his magical enchantments. With her mind clearer, she took a deep breath to steady her racing heart. Her body was at war with itself as she trembled with fear and relief colliding in her core.

The bargain!

She hadn't been able to truly offer Boots assistance because he had told her to do exactly what he said, and he had explicitly told her *not* to rescue any living creature. The faerie had never made explicit that there was an exception should *he* be the one in need of saving. But now he had given his permission for her to help him. Pushing to her feet, Emerlyn lifted her skirts and ran back to her forsaken fare. Bending forward, her fingers wrapped around the dagger's hilt, then she sprinted back to the water.

It was just a few seconds before she saw Boots drinking in a deep gulp of breath, his eyes searching for her. Dropping to her knees, Emerlyn threw herself forward and tossed the blade to his waiting palm. Boots caught the weapon just in time, for it wasn't more than a moment later that he was once again descending down into the depths.

Emerlyn panted as she brought her hands up to cup either side of her face. She wanted to dive in after him, which was absurd. She'd do more harm than good. Watching on, Emerlyn spied a rivulet of crimson weave its way to the top of the water. Biting her lip, she made a wish that the blood wasn't from Boots. She leaned closer, and, for a split second, she was in danger of slipping before her boots found purchase against the soggy grass. Emerlyn began to panic as the blood in her veins chilled. She couldn't swim. As a sheltered English girl, she had never had occasion to learn. Drat decorum and staid rules!

Ever-so-slowly, Emerlyn began to use her elbows to push herself backward. Risking a look behind, she didn't see the nightmare that emerged from the foam before her. When her head was violently yanked forward, strands of her chestnut hair painfully tangled as stabbing sensations pricked her scalp. She screeched with outrage and surprise. Twisting her body around, Emerlyn came face-to-face with a dark-scaled visage, razor-sharp teeth, and beady, black, soulless eyes completely devoid of pupils. The beast opened its huge mouth and screamed at her. Despite Emerlyn's best efforts to keep her eyes open, they squeezed shut as a bursting sensation exploded within her ears. Waiting for a blow to strike or for the creature's teeth to sink into her flesh, Emerlyn kept her eyes forcibly closed.

A blood-curdling wail accosted her senses, and Emerlyn's eyes shot open. The horrid thing was blinking as it looked down on the blade that was speared through its heart. Boots twisted the dagger's handle, then pulled it free, causing a sickening sucking squelch. With lightning speed, he grabbed onto the hand clutching Emerlyn's head and began to saw through it to the bone. It was a horror like she had never witnessed before, but Emerlyn couldn't make herself look away as blood gushed from the growing wound.

"Don't look!" Boots forced through gritted teeth.

Emerlyn was relieved that this was a command she wanted to obey. She couldn't dampen the sounds in her ears, however, so she still heard the relentless melody of steel against bone. It seemed like an eternity, but it was no more than minutes, and the deed was done; the beast had succumbed to the wound to its heart long before the punishing weight of the hand lessened. Emerlyn felt the heat of Boots's body as he rose from the pool, towering over her. Gently, he freed her hair from the dead fingers, taking slow, measured movements to ensure that Emerlyn wasn't hurt during the tiresome process.

"You may open your eyes now," came Boots's whisky-dark voice. A shiver danced up her spine as his moist breath tickled the shell of her ear.

Cautiously, she peeped one eye open, followed by the other. Seeing nothing but her rescuer, her *hero*, if she was being honest, Emerlyn gazed into his golden orbs. She saw relief and something she couldn't quite suss out coalescing together. Butterflies danced in her stomach as an odd tingling made her heart attempt to soar from her chest. Turning her head toward him, she allowed her eyes to rove over his heartbreakingly handsome face.

"Well, now," Boots began, breaking the spell Emerlyn was under. "We shouldn't come across another undine in these waters. They tend to be solitary creatures and fiercely protective of their spaces." He drew away from her. Coming to sit with a *harrumph* and stretching out his legs, Boots gave a barely perceptible wince.

Boots was a sodden mess, the cravat at his neck was lost, and some strange purple water reed clung to his trousers, stained crimson at his ankle. When she noted his hair sticking up in an undignified manner, a giggle escaped Emerlyn's mouth. It was born from equal parts relief and hysteria. She could hardly believe the events that had just taken place and was attempting to wrap her mind around the entire affair. The faerie slowly turned his head toward her as his brows crashed together.

"I seem to have amused you," he said in a far too serious tone. "That was far from my intention. I suppose it's no surprise that my pending demise would entertain you."

Studying his face, her laughter died out in a forced exhale. "Of course, I was terrified for you! I hadn't an idea how to really help you, and then you kept gliding through my fingers, and I couldn't understand why. Despite your loathing of me, I have never truly desired anything but your well-being. I am grieved, sick at heart that you misunderstand my actions. I will say this once, so do listen. I never meant to be the cause of unhappiness for you. Never meant to entrap you. I don't know why, but from the first moment that I saw you, I felt as if you were destined to be mine. It's foolish, I know, but there you have it all the same."

Emerlyn watched his jaw work back and forth as he glared intently at her. He took a deep breath and then jerked. Wrestling with his greatcoat to remove the heavy, waterlogged material, he threw it down to observe the valley of tiny teeth marks marching along his forearm. Drawing in a gasp, Emerlyn reached toward him...to do what she didn't know. Boots wrenched his arm away from her, and her heart splintered into two halves.

"'Tis but a scratch; we faeries heal rather quickly. It won't be more than a bad dream by this time tomorrow. You needn't be so *dramatic* about the matter."

"You can't deny that it pains you," Emerlyn argued, taking care to keep the tremor from her voice. That he was so insistently antagonistic toward her concern created slush to rush through her veins.

"I don't. Simply, I have no need of *your* simpering emotions."

"Oh?" She bristled as his harshly spoken words settled into her broken heart like thorny needles. "Well, do forgive me for displaying concern on your behalf. I shan't bother to do so again!"

Emerlyn never had the urge to strike anyone before, but Boots drove her to unbelievable lengths in her absolute frustration with him as she willed her tightly clenched fist to loosen. She wasn't violent by nature, but his hatred of her drove her in directions she didn't like going. Closing her eyes and pretending he had disappeared, that all of this had been nothing but a nightmare, Emerlyn pretended she was in the parlor, seated before the fireplace with a cup of hot chocolate, watching the tendrils of steam rise. Her shoulder began to relax as the tension melted from her bones, the anger and hurt dissolving into the ether. She couldn't control Boots and had no desire to do so. But she could master her own anger, and maybe in time, he too would grow heartsore of this constant bickering and mockery between them. Emerlyn risked a peek over at him.

Without replying, Boots rose to his feet. His leather boots groaned in protest, before making the oddest slurping sound as he strode over to the basket. His posture was regal, and despite the dripping of his soaked clothing, he looked like he belonged in some king's retinue. Was he a courtier, some knight that had been displaced? How had Boots come to be in her realm? The questions begged to be broached, but Emerlyn didn't have the energy. She found contentment sitting alone as Boots took the time to do whatever it was that was occupying him.

From behind her, the faerie spoke. "We should be on our way, but I think it a very good idea to make camp here for the night. While there are still plenty of daylight hours ahead, I am tired, and I need to heal. How are the blisters on your feet?"

Whirling around, she gaped at him. "How could you possibly know they exist?"

He brought this hand up and ran it down his face, clearly exasperated to have his question answered with another question. "You were limping. It doesn't take one of great intellect to surmise that your boots have left their mark upon your dainty feet."

Emerlyn's face blossomed into a smile as she kicked her feet from beneath her skirts and peered down at them. "You think my feet are dainty, Buttercup?"

"*Buttercup*! These names grow more and more absurd."

"Then give me a name of your own choosing to call you," Emerlyn smirked at him, silently throwing down a metaphorical gauntlet, daring to do as she requested.

"I can't help but wonder whether you know any other letter in the alphabet besides 'B.'"

Bringing her index finger to rest upon her chin, she considered. "Let's start with 'A', shall we? I suppose I could call you Apricot, or Asparagus, or Apple—"

"Do stop with this incessant prattling," he interrupted her with a droning tone.

"Shall I continue with words that begin with 'C'?"

Once again, she smiled up at him. Emerlyn was teasing him and she rather liked that she could annoy and unsettle him. It was only fair, as he seemed to be constantly upending her entire world.

Chapter Four

Chaperone Needed

There was an unsettling pitter-patter rattling around in Alaric's chest. He was very distressed by the discovery. The last thing he wanted was to be drawn into the trap that this discombobulating mortal girl was setting for him. He wasn't supposed to be charmed by her, wasn't supposed to desire her smile or crave the melodic laughter that erupted from her. Alaric had nearly thrown himself back into the current in search of a final ending when he realized that she was a mere breath away, that her delectable lips were ripe for the taking when he had finally freed her glorious tresses.

If he had taken a moment or two longer than necessary to free her, to allow the silky softness to flow over his hands and between his fingers, he could only blame it on the clutch of death that he had felt nearly claiming him. Emerlyn was dangerous to him in so many ways. Clearly, she wasn't a human at all, but a moon goddess or some beguiling enchantress. Alaric wasn't made for her world, and she had no place in his. If he had feelings for her beyond disgust, he could never voice them. What he needed was a chaperone, some being to care for her while he stayed far enough away that her scent of honeysuckle and vanilla wouldn't invade his senses. He'd stay just close enough to ensure her safety, to ensure that he was upholding his end of the bargain. The temptation to grow closer to her, to discover what she tasted like, might dissipate like raindrops in the fog if only he could put some much-needed distance between them.

Alaric wasn't stupid. He knew she felt the pull toward him, had always felt it. But while locked in his Unseelie form, he could easily ignore the sensations battering against his will, seeking to wake his slumbering heart.

Turning away from her, he began the process of preparing the fire to dry his greatcoat. Sinking to his haunches, Alaric meticulously cleared a spot by pulling up the vegetation. The last thing he needed at the moment was to catch the entirety of the area on fire. Emerlyn kept her back to him, gazing upon the waterfall and the enchanting tumble the water took off the craggy rocks. He grumbled under his breath, not wanting to keep an eye on her but realizing should anything happen, he'd be breaking his oath. Alaric needed a calming moment of peace so he closed his eyes and took a deep cleansing breath.

"Stay there," Alaric said as he slowly opened his eyes and rose. His steps carried him toward the lake and the copse of trees stretching their twisty branches high into the air.

"Of course, Cabbage." He couldn't suppress a groan and the curl of his upper lip. Emerlyn was difficult, more so than any human woman or fae he had ever encountered before. By moonlight, the faerie ladies were more agreeable than this idiotic, incapable human *girl.* Yet, he couldn't help the soft grin that bloomed on his face behind his fingers.

Alaric glanced at her over his shoulder, watching her slowly hike up her skirts to remove her half-boots and stockings. Scooting closer to the lip of the water, she stretched her legs before her, dipping her toes in amongst the foam. She slowly moved into the water, allowing the middle of her shins to vanish below the froth. A beaming smile caressed her face, lighting up her expressive dark blue eyes. The sunlight gleamed on top of her head, illuminating the gold highlighting in her brunette hair. She looked so much more womanly without the bothersome bonnet that she chose to wear most of the time. The tilt of her pert nose and the smooth skin of her face begged for the touch of a lover who would cherish and adore her.

Alaric shook his head in an attempt to clear thoughts of her as he gathered fallen timber for their fire.

What a complete fool I am! How could I have forgotten that undine love remote bodies of water? I have grown lax having become accustomed to life over The Wall. We won't survive long in Faerie if I can't remain vigilant. She *won't last long...and I am a faerie of my word, am I not? Emerlyn* will *make it back to her home.*

This foul failure had previously gotten him injured and stuck with his former captor for another day, not to mention that he could still feel sensations of the beast's cruel talons and finned fingers biting into his arms and legs. He shuddered. Faeries didn't desire the touch of others unless they meant something exceedingly precious to them.

But he had borne the soft touches of Emerlyn while he wore the skin of a cat. He'd had little choice in the matter; she had been so insistent that he allow such treatment. The caress of her dainty fingers, the feelings they dragged from the recesses of his soul, had been the most exquisite torture. Even as his skin had flinched and he'd tried to wrangle from her hands, he had craved her. Never once had he bitten or scratched her. There were times even now that the ghosts of her fantom fingers skimmed over his flesh.

He kicked a fallen tree branch, annoyed that all his thoughts kept circling back to the girl. *She's so annoying, aggravatingly so—* he griped. Curiously, he glanced over his shoulder at her, seeing her splash and giggle. *Cute? She's most definitely* not *cute. What in the four realms am I thinking? It has to be exhaustion.*

Alaric snarled, his nose wrinkling and eyes narrowing at himself for those obtuse and absolutely revolting thoughts. He stomped around the outskirts of the wooded area, collecting more branches to last them through the night, and marched back. Alaric threw the wood down in his little clearing, stacking it to make a house, and lit it ablaze with the silver flames of magic that flowed from the open palms of his hands. Holding his greatcoat aloft over the undulating blue flames, it took little time for his outerwear to dry. Pulling it away, he carefully inspected the material.

"Your greatcoat has a hole. Would you like me to mend it?" Emerlyn asked, catching his attention as he straightened. He watched her perched on the craggy water's edge, withdrawing one slender leg after the other, studiously *ignoring* the water droplets that trailed paths down her bare skin.

"I would like for you to be quiet!" he snapped as he commanded his eyes to look elsewhere, hastily redonning his outerwear, his tapered fingers quickly buttoning it.

"I would like for you to be civil, but here we are, Dangleberry."

Alaric growled, striding to stand before her toe-to-toe. The crown of her head barely came to the top of his chest. Emerlyn craned her neck back, glaring at him with those beautiful sapphire eyes that were beginning to haunt him when he closed his own.

"Stop with the incessant repulsive names!"

"No can do, Eggplant. You told me to call you what I please. So I shall."

Alaric swiped a hand over his face. "Must you be so difficult?"

"Must you, Flower? You've hated me since I saved your life. How was I to know what you were? I saw a helpless cat on the brink of death, once Papa had fetched you from nearly frozen water in the depth of winter. And since you've claimed my house was akin to a prison for you, do not forget, it traps me too."

"Psshh," he growled, turning to pace by the fire. "You humans love to manipulate the situation to benefit yourselves."

"How did I manipulate you? I followed what I believed to be my cat into this forbidden realm to *save* him. I suddenly found myself lost and completely stuck when you refused to help me. I had to strike a bargain to gain a modicum of your favor enough to even aid me. If anything, you're crass and cruel!"

"Be quiet," Alaric seethed. "We'll be at the veil in two, possibly three, days time. Can you not be agreeable until then?"

"As you wish, Grape." Emerlyn popped the 'P' in the word grape and squeezed her eyes to slits. Bending forward, she gathered her stockings and boots.

When he made no reply to her, Emerlyn sat beside the fire, setting her footwear down next to her. Bringing her knees to her chest, she arranged her skirts. Within her eyes, anger fused with unshed tears. Alaric grimaced, pivoting abruptly on his heel to avoid the feelings of longing and affection that wanted to take root in his core. Pulling a golden triangular cufflink from his trouser pocket, he flicked it and threw it at the ground; a shimmer of white smoke rose from the grassland, and a turquoise tent materialized through the curling wisps.

Alaric reached out and parted the shelter's flaps, peering inside. Spying his elaborate four-poster bed, along with his other treasured trinkets he had stored prior to his untimely and ill-fated capture by Emerlyn, he sighed. Alaric's head turned, peeking at her over his shoulder, noting her dejected posture. Her head rested on top of her knees as she stared blankly into the ruffling blue flames. His heart squeezed painfully, and Alaric ran his free hand over his chest to soothe the ache within.

"You may take the bed," he said, motioning to the structure's flap and creating a wider opening for her to pass through. Emerlyn continued to stare into the fire.

"Are you deaf?" His temper flared. Alaric was attempting to be *kind* to her. Why must she be so difficult?

"Horseradish, I am not deaf. You told me to be quiet."

"Are you going to go through the entire alphabet?" His exasperation rose higher.

"And then some, Iguana."

Alaric hung his head and his nostrils flared. "Go inside; I will collect our hamper so your stomach doesn't interrupt my rest."

"I am content where I am, Jelly."

"Must you be so vexing? I'm trying to be sincere."

"Oh," she seethed, tilting her head back enough to glare at him. "Is that what you faerie folk call 'sincere?' Forgive me, Kettle, for I am having some trouble learning your dismissive ways. Why bother with kindness when you'll only needle me in a moment or two?"

"Aren't we needling each other, human? You're giving just as good as I have." Alaric's lips firmed together, and he scanned the horizon before he brought his sight back to rest on her. "I propose a truce for the evening. We may even attain some degree of courtesy toward each other. An olive branch, I believe your kind say?"

Emerlyn gave him a brittle smile as she gathered her things and gingerly rose. Brushing past him, she entered his domain. The scent of honeysuckle and vanilla wafted along the air to torture him. Alaric tried to hold his breath as he watched her eyes flit from the cream-colored globe resting on a brass stand to the wooden white pianoforte and matching bench that boasted a scarlet velvet pad. Her gaze landed on the tiered crystal chandelier, casting prisms of light in every direction. The ticking of the ornate mahogany grandfather clock and the decorative bird's nest atop it caught her attention for a moment before the tome-lined bookshelves along one wall held her stare the longest. Emerlyn's mouth formed an 'O', and she turned in a circle. As her delicate toes curled atop the plush navy and daisy-patterned carpet with edged scrollwork, a beautiful smile bloomed across her face.

Alaric's knees went weak. He inhaled and had to swallow to moisten his dry mouth. He thought that he would loathe having her in his home, but witnessing her delight had struck a cord deeply buried within him. He wanted to take her hand and show her each and every feature his tent possessed, but wrinkling his brow and locking his knees, Alaric banished the errant thoughts far away into the recesses of his mind.

He cleared his throat and pointed at the bed where an ivory canopy and matching bedding stood central in the space. "It's not yet evening, but make yourself comfortable. I shall return in a trice with the basket. We have a long night ahead of us, but that doesn't mean we shouldn't take every advantage of the rest that we may." Alaric backed from the tent and took a deep inhale of the fresh air. Separated from her addictive scent, he could breathe much easier.

Chapter Five

How had she, a human girl, found herself in such a setting? Here, Emerlyn stood barefoot on the softest rug in the most luxurious tent while her guide retrieved their dinner. It was bizarre, but this was her life in this unreal moment. Was she blessed or cursed? Emerlyn had certainly felt hexed several times throughout the day. And when that terrifying creature had taken Boots...she screwed her eyes shut as she folded her arms over herself. No, she wouldn't allow those horror-inducing thoughts to have any more room in her mind or heart. Boots hadn't been murdered; he was whole and with her. What a tragedy if ascending The Wall would mean his end no matter what. Boots was only in danger because of her. And, yes, he was difficult, and oftentimes, she wanted to drown him, but the idea of real harm befalling him was not a possibility she could ever live with, even if he hated her.

Would she look back at the time one day and wish she had acted differently? That her words had been softer, her actions kinder? Boots was just such an expert on riling her up. The male made his every move look effortless and graceful. No wonder he was so frustrated by her presence. Emerlyn was like an elephant in a china shop, all bumbling limbs and fumbling words harsh enough to splinter porcelain. A tiny part of her wanted to belong to this world...

Emerlyn's head snapped up as a rustling at the shelter's entrance shifted her attention. Boots breezed into the space and met her stare before he made his way toward her. He held her bonnet outstretched toward her while the hamper swung over his other arm.

"You'll be wanting this tomorrow," he said as the softest light entered his golden gaze.

"T-thank you," she replied, nearly tripping over her words as she tried to suss out what had changed. "Of course, I should have thought to rescue it myself. I don't wish to be more of a bother to you." Emerlyn took it from his hand, gently holding onto the ribbons that dangled from it. Boots nodded at her and carried the basket with their food over to the corner, where a small table sat with just one chair tucked beneath it. Setting it down, he unlatched the lid.

"Feel free to choose what you like. I need a wee bit of rest to restore myself. Sit here at the table while I make use of my bed for a few hours. The books are yours, should you be inclined to delve into them."

Emerlyn did as instructed and sat before leaning over the basket to see what it contained. When she spotted a checkered napkin and what looked like scones, her heart warmed. Scones with a bit of cream and tea were enough to tame any situation and bring even the most dastardly being into civility—or so her father had told her. Setting the napkin and scones down, she frowned. She hadn't thought of her father, not really once, since departing the human realm. She was a terrible daughter. But the freedom that she had been existing under since leaving his house was a balm to her soul. Papa wanted the best for her; she understood that, but his personality was overbearing at the best of times.

When Boots had suddenly disappeared and Emerlyn had discovered the open window, she thought her spirits could not sink lower. But when Papa had asked for her presence in his study and informed her she was to wed their aged neighbor, Sir Hubert, the blood in her veins had turned into a freezing sludge, and her heart had struggled to beat. The decision to set out in search of Boots had been the only salve to her failing heart. Finding him, holding him, when her entire world had come crashing down, was what drove her to the madness of crossing realms. She couldn't bring herself to regret her rash actions. Once returned and married off, Emerlyn would have this adventure to unweave from her memories.

A tear slipped from her eye, slowly trailing down her cheek. She allowed it to flow down her face and plop onto her lap. She was in the process of creating a memory, such as many old women had done when they knew life was going to forever be changed, and a sense in their bones cautioned their life would not be sunshine and roses.

The cadence of snoring roused Emerlyn from her darker thoughts. Lifting her shoulders, she forced herself to smile. She wasn't yet ensconced in a new home with duties to the household and a husband. Twisting her neck, she looked at the sleeping form of Boots spread out upon his bed. His face was turned toward her, the peaceful expression at complete odds with how she normally viewed him. With his dark hair hanging across his forehead, he looked boyish. Emerlyn longed to cross the room to him, to glide her fingertips through his hair, to feel the silkiness and texture. It might be the last time an opportunity ever presented itself. But no, he was not as she had once known him. Back then he hadn't had a voice, but now that he did, and how could she so callously disregard his disgust of her?

The smell of the scones drew her notice and Emerlyn turned back to the basket to search through the various silver tins to find a dollop of cream.

The rippling glow of firelight danced over the plane of Boots's handsome features as he sat beside Emerlyn. A nap had done him a world of good; he was fit as a fiddle. His snide looks and comments had completely fallen away, and she wondered if, perhaps, all along, what he needed to restore his good humor was a rest in his own home.

After a dinner of cold chicken and fresh vegetables, they sat relaxing as their sights rose above them to the darkening sky. Emerlyn was breathless as she watched the teal stars twinkling amidst the orchid background.

"Your appreciation of my world brings a quiet satisfaction to my fae soul," Boots admitted. His dark voice made her skin prickle and she had to force her muscles rigid so she didn't melt into a puddle at his feet.

"Even the most terrifying things here hold some beauty to them, I am discovering," Emerlyn replied as she looked from the stars to him. Tilting her head, her lips curved into a demure smile.

"Is that so?"

"Indeed," she replied and nodded.

"Are you content for the night? I fear I don't have any ladies' clothing hidden away in any of my chests."

He playfully grinned at her.

"Oh, whatever shall I do?" Emerlyn teased back. Then, she subtly brought the collar of her pelisse up to her nose to sniff. Was she in such a disheveled state that she stank? How mortifying, if so! She longed for the earth to part beneath her and swallow her whole.

Boots roared with laughter that startled her, and she very nearly fell forward into the fluttering flames before her. Emerlyn's hands landed on his shoulders, grabbing at his sleeves as Boots's hands molded to her waist. The breath whooshed from her lungs as golden stars danced in her vision. No, they were a set of spectacular golden eyes that were locked in a heated gaze with her own. The scent of sandalwood and his own masculine fragrance invigorated her senses. Emerlyn blinked as the world around her grew hazy, and her heart hammered in her chest. Butterflies were tickling the inside of her stomach with the gentle pressure of their delicate wings. Slowly, Boots drew closer toward Emerlyn, searching her eyes for something she wasn't certain he would find.

When he was a hair's breadth away, Boots spoke. "You are so beautiful. You torture me, and you vex me and make me long for things that are forbidden."

"Sorry—" she winced, remembering that apologies were offensive.

He chuckled before withdrawing his arms from around her. Carefully, Boots captured her hands and removed them from his shoulders, laying them back in her lap. She felt as if she were in a daze, a fog was swirling in her mind as she blinked her eyes. Emerlyn's body became heavier as she sat back on the fallen log. For a moment, she had been weightless, waiting for a kiss that never came. Was she disappointed that he didn't want her? When they were so very different, what did that matter? Emerlyn couldn't keep him; that was bluntly obvious. But oh, with a sinking heart she did discover she desperately wanted to belong to him.

"What do you visualize when you think of your future?" Boots asked, drawing her back to him.

"I don't have to envision it. My father has said I must marry Sir Hubert. I expect when I return, it won't be long until we exchange vows." Her voice wavered as Emerlyn tried to mask her agony over the match.

"That's ridiculous! He's ancient! You would not find happiness with him," Boots's brows careened together as his lips twisted into a scowl.

"Surely, even here in Faerie, you have arranged marriages?"

"It's not uncommon," he admitted with ire.

Emerlyn fell silent as she watched differing emotions play across his face, too fast for her to catalog each one.

"You would want to have children, I daresay." Boots shook his head, not meeting her eyes.

"I did, once. But...sometimes we have to evolve with our dreams, don't you think?" She tried to be positive to hide her fears, but he was drawing Emerlyn's insecurities to the forefront.

"The man beats his horse; I've seen him. What might he do to a wife? You can't be cast off to him." Boots reached for her chin and curled his index finger under it, turning Emerlyn's head to meet his gaze.

"You've been to my world, my home. What choice do I have? No one else has offered; no one else will. Besides, why does it matter to you what shall become of me?"

The faerie before her ground his teeth together as he studied her face, but she suspected that he wasn't really seeing her. Emerlyn's problems were not his to bear. Her longing to belong, to have a love of her own, was not Boots's problem to make right.

Emerlyn sighed, sweeping errant brunette hairs away from her face. She, too, witnessed Sir Hubert's cruel treatment toward animals and really anyone that he viewed as *lesser* than him. It was appalling and heartbreaking. Beyond a doubt, she knew he would take out his frustrations on her, too, should Emerlyn step out of line. She would bear it, more so if they were to have children to whom she'd give her life to protect. It was a dismal future, one she had fled from but knew in her heart that there would be no escaping from.

Emerlyn turned her gaze back to the stars as she let her heart feel all the confusing emotions the evening was evoking. There were none that she wanted to hold onto, none that she dared delve further into.

The vivid colors of this world, so rich and breathtaking, were something she would truly miss. Small pink lights blinked in the distance, hovering around the base of a tree. Emerlyn tilted her head to the side, squinting, curiously watching the lights intently.

"Lightning bugs," Boots stated, pointing toward the trees. "They're harmless."

Emerlyn nodded before turning their conversation to *his* dreams. "What do you picture when you think of your future?"

Boots shrugged, raking his fingers through his tousled black hair. "I'm not certain. I have entertained the notion of traveling to a different realm of Faerie. The Summertide Court has resolved its discourse—"

"No family?" Emerlyn interrupted.

Again, he shrugged. "If circumstances were different...every fae longs for their Fated Mate and for a family. It's not easy for faeries to create faerielings. Little ones are a blessing from the Creator."

"I wish you all the happiness," Emerlyn softly replied. Visions of little ones curling around him, the dimple in his cheek on full display as he held them; it nearly took her breath away. Despite their misunderstanding, she truly believed he would be an excellent father.

Boots smirked, shaking his head. "I appreciate your sentiments."

Emerlyn soured, staring into the flames as sparks of anger zipped along her limbs. "Do you find my sincerity amusing?"

"I find your human ideals interesting, charming even. Fae have never been known to be kind beings. In all the best faerietales, we're always the villains, and I find that's not a label I wish to bear in your story."

Emerlyn's face heated as a blush overtook her. "What role would you wish to play if you were the author?"

He chortled before becoming thoughtful; his lips pulled down into a serious line, his eyes searing into her own. "*Not* the villain."

Rolling her eyes, she gave voice to the thought that began pushing its way further into her mind. "Earlier, you spoke of forbidden things and my hand in making you want them. What was it that you meant?"

Boots's posture stiffened as his lips turned downward. "You must allow me to keep my secrets. I misspoke—"

"But—"

"'Tis time for all faeries and their charges to be slumbering in their beds," he said, rising, extending one hand toward her, waiting for her to take it.

She grasped onto his hand tentatively and rose. There was not even one inch of space between them. Her heartbeat began to race as her blood galloped through her veins, and her imagination wondered just how his lips would feel against hers. She shook her head, dismissing the overwhelming thoughts, and let his hand drop, stepping away from him. Without another word, she turned away and padded into the tent. Dreams were dangerous things in Faerie.

Chapter Six

Frolicking Faeries

Dawn crept across the sky, creating magnificent pinks and oranges that waltzed with the brilliant rays of the rose gold sun. Birdsong rose into the morning, greeting the day. Alaric exited the tent, and glistening dewdrops spotted his black boots as he stepped into the grass. He had left Emerlyn peacefully sleeping in his bed. His night had not been restful on the blankets and pillows he had stacked next to his home's entrance. It had nothing to do with his padded bedding; it was all because of the human girl who bedeviled his dreams. There Emerlyn was, in the forefront of everything he saw, whether his eyes were open or closed. His eyes sought her when he was awake, veering toward her no matter what task he was engaged with. She was there even in his sleep; her face was becoming his ruination even as he craved its sight.

Alaric ran a hand over his aching heart. The more time he spent with her, the harder it would be to bid her goodbye, knowing the bleak future that awaited her. His mood darkened at the thought, and his hands balled into tight fists. The very notion of her wed to the blackguard her father had chosen was–*unfaelievable;* he couldn't even put it into words!

Soft footfalls came from the tent's interior. Emerlyn had risen. His ears picked up the sounds of her pouring water into the washbasin and beginning her morning routine. He knew she wasn't fully dressed; she had made herself comfortable before retiring last eve. Alaric had given her privacy once she had left him standing like a fool before the fire.

He was a fool. He must do better at creating distance between them on today's journey. His heart wouldn't survive were he to completely lose his head.

After a few minutes, when the rustling of redonning her clothes had ceased, Emerlyn peeked her head out from the temporary dwelling's opening, smiling when her searching gaze finally came to rest upon him. "Oh, there you are!" she said as she stepped out of the tent and placed her bonnet atop her head, deftly tying the pale ribbons into a loose bow under her chin."Ready to begin?" she asked; her eyes bright as she scanned the landscape.

"Indeed," Alaric groused as he waved his hand in front of the structure. In a cloud of swirling silver magic, the turquoise tent vanished before them. Alaric opened his hand, and the gold cufflink rested in his palm. Pocketing the trinket, he straightened his greatcoat.

"I did not say anything before, but that was very clever magic to employ. I had no idea that such things were possible," Emerlyn said enthusiastically.

"I'm a faerie; even the lowest of our kind possesses some form of magic. Mine happens to be more elemental. Now, if we are done with today's quizzes, may we be on our way?" He hated that his voice was hard, but it was necessary to ensure no more intimacies occurred between them. It had been an easy endeavor to earn her ire before; he could easily do so again, even if causing her pain carved a bit more of his heart away.

Emerlyn's brows drew together as she bit her bottom lip, looking as if he were a puzzle and wondering whether she held the key to unlock him. He wanted to frighten the possibility away from her mind while simultaneously craving that she unlocked all his secrets.

He strode forth, not waiting for her to catch up as he set a brisk pace. Only the sound of grass being crushed underfoot met Alaric's ears, letting him know she was behind him. They reached the edge of a denser part of the forest and had to weave a trail between the trees as little creatures tried to scurry from underfoot. Even when her breath came in soft pants, he continued in their punishing tread.

Mid-morning came upon them, and Emerlyn's soft voice called to him.

"I need a moment to catch my breath," she gasped out.

Alaric stilled and waited for her to reach his side. Emerlyn's face was pink, and her eyes were shining. His teeth ground together when he discovered that even when she was winded, she was lovely.

How very vexing!

They stood silently as she seemed to relax and draw breaths in more easily. Satisfied that they could continue on, he opened his mouth to address her.

"Look what we have here, Morty!" bellowed a voice from the right of where they stood. Alaric's body stiffened before he stepped in front of Emerlyn shielding her with his body. He scrutinized their surroundings, assessing a path to safety. He could not allow trouble to harm her, the bargain's weight settled onto his shoulders and tightened his heart in a cruel fist.

"What a surprise! Frolicking faeries!" mocked another voice from their left. Alaric's muscles coiled as he thought about the magicked weapons upon his person. One of the pearl buttons attached to his waistcoat would transform into a sword, and he had a crossbow masked as a jeweled pin attached to his greatcoat under the collar. As Alaric lifted his hand to the buttons of his waistcoat, something tackled him from above, crashing him to the forest floor. With an "*ooaf,*" Alaric struggled to push the smelly body from his own as he heard Emerlyn's furious cry.

"Unhand me, you barbarian!" she seethed as struggling sounds rang out.

Air tore from Alaric's lungs as a fist met his stomach, and he doubled over. He coughed and wheezed as he struggled to breathe. Every agonized breath was like fire. His eyes watered, blurring the world from sight, but he couldn't let the bandits take Emerlyn away from him. Alaric swung widely, his fist colliding with something hard as a crack reverberated through the air, followed by a string of curses. Searing pain rippled through his hand at the impact, but he shook it off as he wiped at his eyes and took in the bandit nearest to him, clutching one of his orange-colored eyes.

"Hold still...Hey Morty, this one ain't no frolicking faerie. Its ears are rounded," said one of the brutes, who Alaric thought to be the one faeriehandling *his* human.

A sharp-tipped dagger carved a rivulet of blood to flow into Alaric's cravat. He cringed, thinking of how difficult crimson was to remove from white lace. But having larger problems afoot here, Alaric switched his attention back to the hobgoblin with the blade currently cutting into his flesh.

"Up with you, you rotten carrot!" hissed his attacker, who boasted a swelling eye from having been introduced to Alaric's fist.

A giggle erupted from Emerlyn, and Alaric turned wild eyes to her, scanning her situation, which was not good at all. Her bonnet had fallen to the ground and been stomped upon; her hair was in a disarray of chestnut curls falling over her shoulder and onto her face. The hobgoblin, who wore nothing more than a loincloth, held her down on her knees, staining her dress. He held a short sword firmly pressed against her side, ready to impale her.

"Carrot," she hysterically laughed. "That was not one that *I* had thought of!"

Her captor dug the tip of his sword into her side, and Emerlyn's eyes widened with fright. Her gaze was constantly shifting between the hobgoblins, Alaric, and the weapon. Her face was cleared of any humor, which confirmed her growing anxiety. Since Emerlyn hadn't an inkling of how to charm her way out of the danger with these cantankerous creatures, Alaric needed a moment to sleuth one.

"She thinks I'm funny!" exclaimed Alaric's assailant, sounding chuffed as he preened over Alaric's shoulder, straightening his posture, which angled the blade's tip deeper.

Alaric tried to shake his head in a silent warning to Emerlyn not to encourage the monsters when the dagger bit into him further, causing him to flinch. Alaric grimaced as molten lava rushed through his core. The idea of her coming to harm made red coat his vision, and he had to bite his tongue to stop the roar that wanted to burst from his mouth.

"Well now, fancy seeing you here, Alaric. Last we heard, you had deserted your post. Now we find you here, traipsing around the forest as if you didn't have a care in all the realm." Morty ambled toward him, extending his long, dull, grayish fingers, which gripped a battle ax. When Morty stood before Alaric, he rested the ax against his chest, angling the sharpest point toward Alaric's chin.

"Reckon, there's still a bounty on 'em?" Hobbert inquired from behind Emerlyn, spindly fingers tightening onto her arms. Emerlyn, now silent, recoiled from the pressure. Tears pooled in her eyes.

"Aye, there is." Morty smiled, his breath breaking over Alaric's face, the smell of foul things and excrement making him almost gag. Hobgoblins were the nastiest, ugliest creatures in all of Faerie, even more disgusting was their nauseating breath.

"What do we do with the girl?" Malik's gruff voice asked as his form slinked from the trees to join them.

"I dunno, but I'm sure Major Bartholomeowl will know what's best." Morty withdrew the weapon from Alaric's chest and stepped back a few paces, his scarlet cloak drooping behind him. "Let the girl rise. It'll be dark before we know it, and we've a destination in mind."

"If you harm her, I will eviscerate you," Alaric seethed as his promise coated the air with menace. A faerie promise was a binding, living thing that wasn't enacted lightly, and his promise would see them all dead first. The taste of cinnamon and vanilla wafted into the atmosphere as the words settled heavily over them all.

Morty's eyes locked onto Alaric as he considered him, tilting his head. Bowing at his waist, Morty's free arms swept along the air, creating the vision of a perfect gentlefaeire, which was the complete antithesis of what he was.

Alaric knew that there could be no doubts amongst these imbeciles that Emerlyn meant something precious to him. His captor let his hand with the blade slip to his side, and he gave Alaric a shove to get him to start moving after their leader. Alaric complied when he saw that Emerlyn was on her feet. Hobbert was dragging her along by her forearm, but she was managing to match his gait steadily. She looked more in command of her emotions now, her face serious, and only a shade of panic clung to her eyes. He longed to reassure her that all would be well, but Alaric didn't want to make another promise, especially when he wasn't certain he could keep it. One thing of which he was very confident was that he would die before one hair on Emerlyn's head was injured. That was a vow he silently made to himself. Bargain or not.

Emerlyn took deep, steadying breaths. For the moment, she was safe, yet her hands and feet were bound; she hadn't been seriously hurt, and that was a huge blessing. Alone in the strange little hut, all she could do was listen for scuffling feet. The hobgoblins made such a racket when they walked. Their language was even stranger: garbled shouts intermixed with actual words. Considering all the noise, she wondered how Alaric hadn't heard them approaching since it was known that fae had excellent hearing. What has taken his focus from their safety?

Sitting up, Emerlyn gazed around her. The hut was crude, allowing beams of light through the cracks. She breathed in deeply again, taking in gulps of fresh air that wasn't tainted by the stench of the hairless horrors. When Emerlyn had first laid eyes on the hobgoblins, she had nearly released her bladder. When she had been kneeling on the forest floor watching her protector try to fight their way to freedom, her terror had grown vicious claws that savaged her insides. She could not lose him...

Holding her hands up, Emerlyn inspected the knots holding her palms together. Biting her bottom lip, she pondered whether she wanted to risk her teeth to bite through the rope. She felt hopeless and afraid for Alaric.

Alaric...the name suited him. It was a very beautiful name, and it was absolutely undeniable that he was a very beautiful faerie. What did he see when he looked at Emerlyn? Her skin wasn't smooth like that of a fae. Her hair didn't have the natural shine, and her eyes didn't hold mysteries in them. She was just too...ordinary, too *human*. Emerlyn had no idea how or even if she was going to be rescued. Supposing that ending up in the belly of some fae creature was better than a life married to Sir Hubert. Emerlyn sighed, closed her eyes and attempted to rest; there was nothing else to do, captive as she was. Perhaps a happily ever after wasn't something she was destined for, no matter which realm she was in.

Chapter Seven

Dining Delights

Alaric sat straighter in his chair as he watched Major Bartholomeowl prowl into the cottage. He wouldn't display the panic that was making his heart rate trill or show the sweat that dampened his palms. What Alaric needed the most was control over his mind and emotions to best the cunningly brutal faerie. He had not allowed himself to crack under the savagery and scrutiny of the two hobgoblins who had dragged him in and stood at the sides of the entrance, their squinty eyes locked on his every breath.

The Major found the chair opposite Alaric and pulled it from under the table to sit. He folded his arms across his chest as his beak twisted into a smile filled with mockery. A calico tail rose up behind the half-cat-like body dressed in military regimentals. Large yellow eyes set in a downy owl head took in every detail about his opponent.

"Having a tiresome day?" Alaric ventured to begin the conversation.

"It's grown much more entertaining in the last few hours with your unexpected return. You do recall the punishment for abandoning the cause?"

"I never abandoned *my* cause. I was captured and unable to see it through," Alaric stated with a coldness that paraded his contempt.

"As you say. How about a drink, old friend?" The Major rose and walked to the sideboard that held bottles of various shapes containing liqueurs in an array of colors. Selecting one of dark amber, he poured a fingerful into a glass tumbler and brought it to the table, placing it down before Alaric.

Lifting his bound hands, Alaric shook them before replying, "I must decline."

"Too bad, it's a fine vintage *procured* from the king's personal pantry."

A knock on the cottage door sounded.

"You may enter," the Major called out.

Hobbert appeared through the open doorway once again, this time dragging Emerlyn by a forearm. Bruises littered her bare arms, and he felt a zap of lightning strike his heart. It had to have been done to her before his promise had been made; else, they couldn't have hurt her. Alaric's eyes cataloged the rest of her, seeing that Emerlyn was freshly bathed and wearing a new empire-waisted dress in cornflower blue. Tiny embroidered white flowers graced its hemline and the edges of the puffed sleeves. Matching satin slippers peeked from beneath her dress. Emerlyn's hair was left to loosely hang, caressing her neck and curling down her shoulders. Alaric's fingers itched to weave their way through the shining tresses.

"Ah, so *pleased* you could join us this evening, my dear," Major Bartholomeowl greeted her with an oily smile.

A rough shove against the middle of her back almost had Emerlyn tumbling to the wooden floor, but their host was there to catch her. Clasping onto her elbow, the Major steered her toward a chair at the end of the rectangular table. Hobbert received a cutting glare from his leader before sauntering over to stand sentry along the wall.

"A pleasure," she answered, sitting down and meeting Alaric's eyes. He saw relief and wariness warring in her gaze. Alaric gave her a slight smile, attempting to reassure her all would be well. He needed her to believe him...believe *in* him.

Retaking his seat, the Major clapped his paws, and in came four male faeries with laden dishes topped with silver domes. A small faerieling followed with a giant candelabrum, which he struggled to place down in the middle of the table. When he managed his task and backed away, the servers set the dishes down, removing the lids that revealed savory scents and wavy tendrils of steam. The faeries retreated from the cottage, the door gently closing in their wake.

Set before the trio were roasted hog beasts dripping with a brown sauce, creamed artichokes with cubed potatoes, and a tureen of creamy soup with diced bits of onion and chives floating on top.

"Do dig in," the Major purred, looking decidedly like the cat who had gotten the cream despite his hooked bird beak.

Alaric cast Emerlyn a quick look, begging her not to eat whatever was in front of her. Emerlyn glanced between him and the Major, straightening her back as her eyes pinched.

"I do apologize, but I'm quite full," she softly told the Major.

The faerie barked a laugh. "Oh, are you? Then shall we cease formalities and cut to the chase?"

"*Please* do, as this is quite suffocating," she hissed, ire lacing her tone.

Alaric quirked a smile, finding her use of a faeriely offensive word with her irritated tone to be quite amusing, especially when it was directed his way. The Major's eyes flared before sliding from the crown of her head to her well-displayed cleavage the dress revealed. Black speckles dueled across Alaric's vision as his blood heated. The lout had no right to look at Emerlyn in that way. No being, faerie, nor human had that right.

"*Indeed*," the Major replied.

Emerlyn leaned forward. "*Thank you*." Was she aware that she was putting her assets on more of an exhibit for the cretin? She was playing a dangerous game.

Alaric sucked in his lips and stared at his lap, trying to compose himself as the tips of his pointed ears betrayed his festering rage. He hoped his face conveyed his absolute horror and disbelief to her. If she wasn't trying to kill him with various ridiculous names, he was certain she would try to murder the Major with politeness mingled with a fair dose of feminine wiles.

"Leave the human out of this since she has yet to grasp our ways," Alaric began nonchalantly. "Your unprecedented tiff is with me."

The Major beamed, revealing rows of pointed teeth. "You would like me to, would you not?"

"Please show me a modicum of kindness and allow Alaric to take me back to my human realm," Emerlyn pleaded, batting her long sooty eyelashes. "If you would, I would be forever *thankful*."

The Major's eyes glimmered with a threat as he growled in contemplation. Alaric used the moment to gently break the thread holding the third pearl button of his waistcoat in place. He allowed the fastener to rest against his closed palm, ready to strike when the time was right.

"How about a dance, and I might consider allowing you your freedom. Of course, I can't let Alaric slip past my defenses again. But you, I could part with once you gift me with a dance." The Major winked at Emerlyn and was astounded when she flashed him a teasing smile in return.

"I can agree to your request, happily enough. Do you fancy a polka or perhaps—" she began.

"No, no, no, my dear. You misunderstand my meaning. I require you to dance *for* me while I have the pleasure of watching you."

The smile slipped from her face as her eyes turned to Alaric. He had to bite the inside of his cheek to keep from tearing the man to minuscule specs.

How dare he!

Alaric saw fear swimming in her eyes. At the moment, he was powerless to do anything. He could not jeopardize their chance at freedom. Swallowing, Alaric nodded, though he felt like his inaction was a betrayal to his vow to keep her safe. The last thing he desired was for Emerlyn to debase herself, but what choice did either of them have?

Rising, Emerlyn stood in place and looked around the room. "There doesn't seem to be any music."

"Hum, you can do that, can't you?" The Major asked in a tone dripping with condescension.

Emerlyn scooted her chair backward and then softly trod to the middle of the room where there was more space. Her cheeks were stained cherry as her eyes lowered to the bare floor. Softly, she began to hum a melody Alaric had never before heard; her hips swayed in one direction and then swiveled to another. Her arms extended outward as her feet took turns propelling her back and forth before she twirled on the tips of her slippers in a circle, loose hair sweeping behind. Emerlyn was glorious and it made the barbs in his chest sink in further. He wanted to get up and close the distance between them to shield her body from the view of the leering brutes in the room. He wanted to jump to his feet and pluck the eyes from every faerie present. But he couldn't do either of those things.

Across from him, the Major sipped from his goblet. His entire attention was fixed on his dancing puppet, eyes burning with eagerness. Grinning vilely, the Major rose from his seat, crossing the expanse to Emerlyn. His furry hands wrapped themselves around Emerlyn's waist.

Alaric saw red. Crushing the pearl button in his hand, his sword materialized. In a fluid motion, he cut his bindings and charged headlong toward Major Bartholomeowl. The devilish fiend shoved Emerlyn away; the rough action caused her to fall with a shriek as she skidded across the wood floor.

"You'll never make it out," the Major growled, eyes alight with menace and cruel promises.

"On the contrary," Alaric rebutted, their weapons crossing. Alaric shoved the Major off, striking defensively and earning a blow on the Major's shoulder. "*You* won't."

The Major howled, charging back. Appendages stiff from being bound, Alaric struggled to keep the beastly man at bay. He parried a blow meant to take off his head, twirled around, and landed on a dining chair. The hobgoblins in the room charged forward, crude weapons striking the air. Alaric leaped over one, his sword finding flesh in a hobgoblin's back. Landing on his feet, he struck down two more nasty creatures as he made his way closer to Emerlyn.

The doomed Major slipped off to Emerlyn, grabbing her about the waist and lifting her off her feet. The unfaely creature lugged her backward toward a closed door. Alaric roared, cutting down the other hobgoblins with ease. His once tense muscles loosened, now finding a rhythm in which to dispatch his enemies.

"How much do you fancy your human, Alaric Moonfur?"

Growling low, Alaric closed the distance in the blink of an eye, his faerie strength lending him aid. Alaric dared not make eye contact with Emerlyn, not when their lives depended upon his success. His sword was angled down at the Major's head. The bloodthirsty scoundrel thrust Emerlyn in front of him. Using a free hand, Alaric grabbed onto her middle and swung Emerlyn out of the way.

The two opponents glowered at each other as their swords danced. Metal clashed, steel on steel rang out in the air creating a din akin to thunder. Major Bartholomeowl leaped over Alaric, kicking him mid-air which had him gasping, and launching him backward. Alaric crashed to the floor, sliding across the rough wooden planks. Emerlyn's gasp was like a knife to his heart. He vaulted to his feet, charging headlong.

The Major, grinning like a fiend, gnashed his teeth together, before taking an athletic stance in fervid anticipation. Alaric grinned back, sliding on the floor and swiping the legs out from under the haughty fool, whose weight thundered against the floor, reverberating along the walls. Regaining his feet, Alaric pounced, shoving his blade through the middle of the Major's throat.

Major Bartholomeowl heaved a gurgle before staring vacantly at the ceiling. Alaric withdrew his bloody sword from the villain's throat, wiping the gore from his blade across the dead faerie's body.

"Don't look," Alaric whispered, taking Emerlyn gently by the hand, gripping it tightly. "We must flee!"

"I will follow you anywhere, *Alaric*," she solemnly told him.

Their eyes met, so many differing emotions passing through each, and he leaned toward Emerlyn and pressed a warm kiss to her forehead. Taking a moment, he breathed her in and felt as if his heart still resided in a vise. He could so easily have lost her. He led her toward the door where a cloak stand stood. Letting her hand go, he removed a drab gray cloak that reeked of rotted onions and cabbage. When he wrapped it around her, securing the hood over her head, Emerlyn's nose wrinkled in disgust.

"It's the best I can do at the moment," he trailed off as he crept to the door and carefully opened it.

"No need to apologize, *Alaric*," she teased as she moved to stand behind him.

Canting his head back toward her, he smirked, then shook his head. Hearing his name upon her lips was like a wave crashing against the sand in a hurricane. His battered sense gave way to determined focus. Now was not the time to let down his guard. Peering through the crack in the door, he waited a moment and took stock of where the other guards were. A massive bonfire took up the middle of the area, where the ugly creatures danced and drank from their tankard of ale. None were paying the least bit of attention to them. The stars were watching out for them, and under their sparkle, Alaric opened the door wider. Taking Emerlyn's hand, they raced from the cabin and straight for the trees.

Chapter Eight

Dancing on Air

The stitch in Emerlyn's side was nothing in comparison to the ache of her feet. Fleeing for one's life over a deciduous forest floor wasn't kind to silk slippers. She might as well have been barefoot. Still, she wouldn't allow herself to complain. She was out of danger, at least for the moment. Alaric expertly guided her, his fae eyesight being far superior to hers. As long as her legs kept up, she was safe enough to ponder the tender kiss and all that had happened before in that stifling cottage.

She'd been surprised by the new dress and the offer of a bath. Once untied, Emerlyn balked when her jailor only turned his back to her while she cleaned herself. She had quickly seen to her tasks and, once bedecked, she found herself standing in the same dwelling as her bargain mate. All of her pent-up anxiety melted from her bones to see that Alaric was unharmed and whole. While she wanted to flee to his side, she knew that what was to come would determine their fate and she would not jeopardize their lives or freedom by such a silly action. Besides, he didn't feel drawn to her as she did to him. *But the kiss...*

When Emerlyn had been ordered to dance like a woman of the night, she knew she had no choice but to accept her fate. Not only was her life being threatened, but the idea of watching something befall her traveling companion when they were both relatively unscathed, made it an impossible situation. After all, hadn't she been baiting the leader, refusing to back down against the tyrant? She had pushed her luck as far as she could. So Emerlyn danced even though it was an intimate setting, and all the eyes upon her, save her rescuer, were ogling her. Emerlyn had pretended she was alone in the safety of her ballroom with none to witness the way her body moved to her own hummed melody. It had worked. When she had found herself falling, Emerlyn couldn't stem the cry that erupted from her. And when *Alaric,* her champion, had felled every soul in that cottage, she hadn't been one wit frightened. It was as if the stony and contrary demeanor of the faerie Boots had vanished, and in his place was a hero that any lady would swoon over. And she nearly had! That kiss had melted her knees into pudding.

"Just a bit further, and we can slow our pace," Alaric told her in between panting breaths.

Emerlyn only nodded, too winded for much more.

Chiming bells filled the air around them, and the trees began to thin out, their golden-leaved branches giving way to patches of the night sky. Floating faerie lanterns drifted above their heads while little wooden houses hung from individual strings of silvery webbing.

A few more steps brought the pair to the center of the glade, where a band of elves were making music with instruments and their high-pitched voices. They wore what looked like canary-hued moss, and large leaves were in differing shades from gold to bronze, and even a few smaller silver star-shaped leaves. The long, bedraggled beards that flitted with the breeze were auburn, gray, or white. The eyes that landed on the couple were all the same—smallish with jade brilliance and rimmed in inky lashes. If all had been made to stand in a row, each tiny man would have risen no higher than Alaric's knee.

"Visitors, Brother!" one elf said as he set his fiddle aside and thumped his neighbor beside him.

"I see that Brother!" answered the second one as he set his flute down beside the fiddle.

"We do so like visitors!" piped up the third elf with an auburn beard and looked to be the youngest of the clan. He lay the lyre atop his lap.

"Welcome to our home, strangers!" boomed an elf with the whitest and longest beard amongst them. He had no instrument, but he had been singing before the group had abandoned their song. When the elf waved his hand to encompass the land, his fingers were twisted at odd angles and looked arthritic and painful. Emerlyn's fingers twitched in sympathy to his plight.

"We are pleased to wander into your enchanting home," Alaric replied, smiling as he stood in place beside Emerlyn.

Was it a trick of the light, or was his smile especially beguiling this moonlit eve? Emerlyn's heart fluttered as a slight blush rose to her cheeks. He mustn't discover the effect he had on her, not when he was taking her home...

"Rest yourselves and stay the night here under our protection," offered the one who had welcomed them.

"We will," Alaric said, then bowed his head to their group.

Emerlyn looked closer at the elves and spotted close to thirty of them sitting on logs or blankets. There were females who sat further back and had been hidden by the ones who had first caught their attention. The ladies were seated on chairs with lattice backs and periwinkle cushions. All clothed in dresses with the same leaves and moss, they also wore little matching pointed hats, and the tips of their wooden shoes were each topped with a flower. Daisies, violets, and carnations peeked from beneath their hemlines.

"You must be famished, my poor dears," said a little lady elf, rushing from her chair to a table located off to the side. Her deft hands quickly selected a basket with a cream napkin on top of it. When she made her way toward them, Emerlyn noticed that her back bore a slight hunch along the spine. Wisps of white hair escaped from her hat, giving her a harried appearance, but her kindness was genuine, and she made Emerlyn's fears abate.

Alaric took the basket from the elf's hand, nodding to her. What a shame it was to never be able to express one's gratitude; it was stupid, really. Alaric tugged Emerlyn's hand, which he still had yet to let go, and she walked beside him a little distance to a clear space where a single log lay. Sitting down, they looked in the basket laden with freshly baked bread, cheese, and some fruit that looked like grapes but were a pale pink in color. He allowed her hand to drop from his now that they were stationary and relatively safe.

"'Tis fine to eat whatever catches your eye," Alaric assured her, handing out a huge chunk of the bread to her.

Emerlyn had no reason to doubt Alaric. He would've cautioned her not to satiate her hunger if the act would doom her to residing in Faerie. Taking the flakey crust from him, Emerlyn frowned. Yes, she was starving, but she didn't feel like eating. What she longed for the most was a way to stay in Faerie, even though it had proven dangerous for her. This was living, and Emerlyn wanted to taste every moment of her life, not rot away in some antiquated man's home. What she most wanted was to remain by Alaric's side. Despite his kiss earlier, he didn't want to keep her; he had been attempting to be rid of her since he regained his strength in her realm. Like a fool, she had seen something, felt something that didn't exist.

They ate without exchanging any words, watching on as the elves sang and played their instruments. When Emerlyn was near to bursting from the sweet juices of the fruit, the elves began to clear the chairs away. Groups of two paired off, and dancing began as the music's gentle notes swelled into the evening air. It was a Scottish reel, she realized as she bit her lip. She had never been asked to dance one before but had watched the villagers at home kick up their heels. Feeling eyes upon her, Emerlyn switched her attention to a young elf with curly auburn hair and a matching beard that barely grew past his neck. He walked to her eagerly and bowed.

"Would you like to dance?" he asked; a sparkle twinkled in his eyes.

Emerlyn nodded her head, having no idea how this was to work with their height difference but not wanting to miss out on this adventure. She rose to her feet. The elf came to her thigh and took her hand in his. Leading her to an open spot, the little man let go of her hand and began intricate footwork that moved his body gaily around her own. Emerlyn smiled and bent forward, gaining her hemline, and twirled in place. From the corner of her eye, she spotted a younger female elf approach Alaric. Emerlyn guessed that he, too, had been asked to dance. Alaric rose and allowed the lady to lead him off. When the notes died down, Emerlyn allowed her dance partner to tug her toward Alaric and his lady.

"Time for a dance with my sweetheart," her partner said, letting her hand go and reaching for the hand of Alaric's partner. The lady's tanned cheeks turned scarlet as she ducked her head and allowed herself to be whisked away.

Alaric watched the pair for a moment before turning back to Emerlyn. He brought his hand up and clutched the back of his neck.

Is he nervous? Whatever for?

Clearing his throat, he asked, "Would you like to... um...dance? You don't have to; it's not a demand." He was quick to add the last part, seeming to hold his breath, awaiting her answer.

She wanted to! Oh, how she wanted to when they weren't averting disaster and fleeing for their lives. The desire to be enclosed in his arms was like a hunger eating her from the inside out.

"Yes, that would be lovely," Emerlyn answered as she tried to keep the excitement at bay. But she couldn't mask the delight in her eyes or the hammering of her heart rushing the blood from her veins to heat her face.

Alaric's face flourished into a smile that reached his eyes, lighting them up. Her breath seized in her lungs. She had never been the focus of such a male before, and he had never looked at her in this manner before. It was as though she had been residing in a dungeon all her life, and he had just broken all the locks of the very cell that had held her captive. If Alaric had asked her to grow wings and fly away with him, she thought that maybe she could. Emerlyn was light as a feather on her feet as he encircled her waist and gently clasped her hand, steering their feet into the beginning of their dance.

The notes of the music never reached her ears. It was as if only Alaric and she existed, tethered to each other by some ancient magical force. Where his body began and hers ended, she didn't know, couldn't tell. Their breaths mingled together as they maintained their pace. She wondered if a hurricane could tear their locked gazes away because it wasn't within her power to do so. How could she go the rest of her life not feeling this way? To never be held like this again? To never feel as if she danced upon the air? The world came crashing down when a voice interrupted the palace they had created together and filled with all the thoughts unspoken.

"The hour is late, my friends, and all must be now abed as the Sandman draws near." Emerlyn stood still for a moment, blinking, attempting to gather herself and vault her heart back up into her chest.

"Of course," she heard Alaric murmur.

"We've made accommodations ready in two separate tents, just there." The elf pointed, and Emerlyn followed his finger in that direction. Side by side were two blush tents large enough for the two of them.

"Splendid," she heard herself remark. Allowing Alaric to lead her toward their dwellings, she couldn't help but feel that every step carried them away from a place they may never find their way back to.

Alaric drew the tent flap aside and peered inside, then faced her before nodding his head. "I shall see you tomorrow, Emerlyn, rest well."

"Rest well, *Alaric.*"

Ducking through the opening, her eyes didn't really see the navy bedroll or the small lantern beside it. Her arm was extended behind her, attached to Alaric's hand. Emerlyn couldn't bring herself to turn around and bid him a goodnight, not when the next time it would be a final parting. Her ears caught his heavy sigh as he let her hand go, and then he was gone. The rustling sounds of the canvas haunted her long into the night, becoming a chorus to the hooting of an owl.

Chapter Nine

At Last, An Escort

After a breakfast tasting of cinders, it was time to begin their final leg home. She would be under her father's eaves in the late hours of the evening. Would Papa's words be harsh or soft at her absence? If given the chance to make the journey all over again, she wouldn't change one moment of it, even the frightening and humiliating ones. Emerlyn had grown leaps and bounds in just a few short days, forever changed, and she welcomed the new version of herself. She had created some very treasured memories and would draw them out whenever she needed an escape. Were it not for this adventure, she wouldn't have such...but what could she name her memories? Heartwarming, exciting? And more. So much more. For how many mortal women could ever admit to dancing beneath a turquoise moon in a bespelled forest with a faerie who took her breath away? She was lucky, she told herself. But she didn't feel lucky to be leaving this all behind. To bid her rescuer a forever farewell.

Beside her, Alaric rose and held out his hand for her to take. When she was standing at his side, the leader of the elves, Errok, joined them.

"I understand your journey back to The Wall will be lengthy. I have called upon a friend who has agreed to assist you," Errok informed them, as a wide smile crinkled the umber skin surrounding his eyes. "Stardust, would you mind gracing us with your esteemed presence?"

Through the trees, a horse with a coat as white as an English pearl whinnied as it trotted forward. Holding its head high, the dazzling silver horn atop its head glinted in the luminous sunlight, casting glimmers of rainbowed light to the delight of Emerlyn's soul.

A unicorn! Prancing right before her! When she had seen the nightmarish creatures of this realm, how could she have forgotten about all the legends illustrated on the pages of her favorite tomes? She felt her heart rate pick up as her skin pebbled, and euphoria rushed through her.

Stardust came to a halt before them, bowing his regal head. Emerlyn dropped into a curtsy. When she rose, the teal eyes of the magnificent stallion were staring at her with open curiosity. When his gaze moved to study her eyes, Emerlyn matched his gaze, giddy that she was interesting to him. Stardust certainly exceeded any wild imaginations her mind had ever produced; why, even his hooves seemed to sparkle with magical dust. *Stardust.*

"I sensed there was some faerie in need of my services. I am happy to allow you to ride upon me as we traverse the dangerous wilds that lead to The Wall. Shall we begin the journey?" Stardust looked at Alaric, awaiting his reply.

"Yes, I do believe that would be wise." Alaric captured Emerlyn around the waist and agilely lifted her onto Stardust's back. Emerlyn muffled her exclamation of surprise by pressing her lips firmly together. His hands were removed before she could really enjoy the sensation of being held by Alaric. Before disappointment could prickle her heart and settle into her marrow, Alaric leaped to his seat behind her. Solid arms enclosed Emerlyn, and she tilted her body against his muscular chest and sighed. The fragrance of sandalwood mixed with his essence encompassed her, creating a feeling of security that settled along her body like a well-loved blanket.

"Don't forget the basket my missus packed for you," Errok said, lifting the basket above his head.

Alaric extended his arm and grasped onto the handle, hauling the basket to his side, where it hung from the crook of his elbow.

"We are so very—" Emerlyn began. "Grateful for you and your many kindnesses." She was human, after all, and some things were too ingrained for her to appreciate them in herself. Humans expressed their thankfulness, and she resolved that the fae could just deal with it. If they found her peculiar, so be it. Emerlyn didn't mean one ounce of disrespect.

Errok threw back his head and laughed. The sound startled Emerlyn and her body gave a lurch forward as her eyes widened. Her hands latched onto the strong arms around her, anchoring her.

"You are a breath of fresh air for these old bones, Emerlyn. Be true to yourself, do you hear me? Those that matter don't mind, and those that mind have no place in your sphere. Take care, my friends, and if the Creator is willing, we shall cross paths again."

Emerlyn smiled at the elf even though tears sprang to her eyes. She had chosen to follow her heart, and it hadn't steered her wrong.

"Until next time, Errok," Alaric bowed his head.

With a nod of his head to Errok, Stardust began an even trot. Within moments, the trio was moving through the trees much faster than before.

Scrunching her brows together, Emerlyn made herself ask Alaric one of the questions that had been plaguing her since her eyes first opened that morning. "Where did you learn to sword fight?" Perhaps he wouldn't answer her. Would that surprise her? No, there was a tidal wave of things Emerlyn didn't know about him, and she wondered if Alaric would ever allow her to dip into those waters.

"Training, Emerlyn...," he faltered, then started again. "I serve at the pleasure of the king. I've been one of his personal guards for decades."

"Decades?" Emerlyn squeaked as a glacier coasted over her skin, chilling her to the bone.

"As I said. I was sent on a mission to ferret out some information, and that is how I came to know the Major and his disreputable regiment."

"A spy mission!" Emerlyn exclaimed in an awe-filled voice. Things were starting to come together for her. He would have been a spectacular spy and an even better personal servant to the Faerie King.

Alaric continued, "Indeed. But things went awry as they often do under the Major's command, and the prey I was sent after climbed over The Wall, which left me with little choice but to follow. After hunting him for days, we clashed. And though I was injured, he succumbed to his fate."

"Oh, dear." She leaned her head back to look up at him. His lips curved as he stared down at her. "And Papa found you in your feline form."

"I found that once I was in your world, the compulsion to transform was undeniable. Anytime I even attempted to change back, it was impossible because I had been in your realm for too long."

Silence stretched between them, encapsulating each one in their own thoughts. Even Stardust remained mute. They trotted along for a few hours as the sky slowly fluctuated from the muted tones of dawn to the more defined pinks and purples of midday.

Some creature whizzed by Emerlyn's ear and then came back toward her face. Brilliant orange eyes set in an orchid body of feathers flapped its wings to keep their pace. Bringing her hand up, Emerlyn allowed the tiny hummingbird to settle into the palm of her hand. Gently rubbing its head against her bare skin caused a smile to bloom upon her face. Leaning toward her palm where the bird rested, for she didn't dare move her limb in case the action spooked the fowl, she was better able to observe it. The winged creature leaped from its perch, rubbing its chest along her nose. Emerlyn chortled with delight, her heart bursting with affection for the little bird. It was the most precious being she'd ever held in her hand. The bird soared above her head, disappearing in the canopy of golden leaves.

"Do your charms know any boundaries?" Alaric teased, but she heard the note of a smile amongst his words.

"She's completely captivated me," Stardust admitted, craning his neck to look back at the pair atop his back, giving Emerlyn a wink.

A blush was quick to rise to Emerlyn's skin as she ducked her head. The unicorn faced forward again.

"I don't believe I charm every being I meet. You are a perfect example of that." Emerlyn bit her lip as bumblebees darted around her stomach.

"I must admit to being enchanted by you."

"But not in your feline form?" Emerlyn asked, for she truly was curious to know how he had felt about her. *Really* felt. She knew all of his blistering accusations, but were they true even now?

"There were times when I was quite content. But still, the feeling of entrapment lingered."

"I am so sor—"

"Do not. We have been over this and your apparent obsession with offering useless apologies," Alaric blustered, and she felt him shift his body weight.

While he was already annoyed at her, she might as well push him further. "Must I return? Is that truly what you wish?"

"What I wish doesn't matter!" Anger lined his words, making Emerlyn draw her shoulders forward.

"Why not?" she demanded. If this was to be, she wanted a very clear reason why. Didn't she deserve that?

"I serve at the pleasure of the King of all Faerie! I never know when I shall be assigned to rescue the realm. Or when travel plans will be made for me. My life is not my own." His words rang with a hollowness that neatly cleaved her heart into two halves.

"I could find employment as a maid or—"

"*I* am a soldier, Emerlyn. I cannot stay in the palace to protect you!" Alaric bit the words out from a clenched jaw.

"I am not wholly powerless! Besides, may I not barter for holly berries or some other form of protection?" Emerlyn desperately searched for a solution, clinging to any hope, any possibility.

"There are no certain protections; some fae are too clever and will delight in finding ways around—"

"How can you accept that? How can you just be content to take me home and walk away?" Emerlyn didn't try to stem the tears that spilled from her eyes, down her cheeks, and straight to the backs of his hands that were around her. Alaric tightened his grip around her, remaining silent and still as marble. How she wished that the mere action could keep all of her broken bits safely tucked away.

Chapter Ten

Home

Never in his long-lived life had Alaric ever hated silence. It had always been his friend and ally. But when it stood in the air—his greatest foe yet—separating him from his...he couldn't bear its presence.

Miles had been gained in the hours since Emerlyn's sobs had blessedly ceased. He didn't feel any less a villain even though total silence enveloped them. Not even Stardust dared to break the oppressive atmosphere. It wasn't the unicorn's place to make this right. It could never be made right. Ribboned pieces of his heart were barely staying together, and each breath he took threatened to sever the organ completely.

The trees thinned, giving sight to the stony wall. His heart leaped into his throat as bile burned a course up from his queasy stomach. Alaric would have much rather stood before an executioner than follow through with this mission. He was lost in the churning of his mind when Stardust's gait halted.

Emerlyn's hands landed on his, tugging them from her. Alaric's fingers wanted to dig in and hold her tight, but he pulled away from her, dropping to the ground beside the unicorn. Before he could reach for her, Emerlyn was slipping from Stardust. Catching her, Alaric guided her to her feet. Emerlyn turned, casting her eyes away from him, and addressed their escort.

"Thank you, Stardust." Emerlyn's voice was raspy from her tears.

"It was my pleasure," Stardust told her as his foreleg bent, lowering himself into a courtly bow.

Not sparing Alaric even one last look, she softly padded toward The Wall. He didn't doubt that she could climb it; she had done so before. She was made only stronger by her time in Faerie...

Alaric rubbed a hand over his wounded chest and watched her go as his world crumpled at his feet. His heart was screaming, begging him to end this torture. How would he pass his days without her? What would fill the endless hours of his years besides duty?

"You still have time. Go after her. You can figure out all the rest later," commanded Stardust with an impatient shake of his head. "Your duty is to your heart."

Alaric stood dumbfounded. Could this have been a test from fate? If he took this leap, would the Creator provide a way for them? He would never know unless he tried! Hope lit his chest with a warm glow. She was his everything, and he couldn't let her go.

"Wait," he called out. "Emerlyn, *please!*"

It was the plea in his voice that stopped her. But she didn't turn to face him. A tremor wracked her slim frame, and he longed to pull her into his arms. But first, he needed to give voice to his thoughts.

"You have my *humblest apologies* for denying what this is between us. You could not have known, had any idea, that you are my Fated Mate. I will not fight it any longer. I cannot. My dearest Emerlyn, you are my moon and sun, my most precious jewel. My everything. I have lived and fought for my kingdom for decades. Tonight, I choose to fight for myself. What *I want* is to be *yours*. What I have *craved* since the moment we met, as your arms held me to you, is the taste of your lips. Tell me I am not too late! Tell me that you forgive me." Alaric was stunned not only by the words flowing from his soul but also by the lone tear falling from his eye. Faeries didn't cry. It was too beneath them.

"Is this some trick? Some last vestige of your loathing of me?" cried Emerlyn.

He let out a keening wail at the thought that she even had to ask how genuine his words were. Shaking knees barely held him up, but Alaric stood solidly before her as she cautiously faced him. Emerlyn's eyes bore into his own, searching them as if they were the window to his soul. What had she discovered that made her run straight into his arms? He caught her, swinging her around in a wide circle and breathing in the sweet scent of honeysuckle and vanilla. Alaric withdrew a hand from her waist and grazed his knuckles across the side of her satiny cheek. This was where he was meant to be.

Emerlyn lovingly met his gaze as she spoke, "I will have you with all of my heart. I've always been yours, you frustrating faerie." A smile lit up her face; her eyes shone with pure love and adoration.

Alaric erased the fraction of space between them, kissing the tip of her nose. "Stardust, would you take us home?"

"*That* would be my pleasure! Where is 'home'?" Stardust's teal eyes sparkled in the moonlight.

"The palace will do quite nicely. I have a position to negotiate. The king is in need of advisors who have actually *seen* his kingdom." Alaric had been a faithful friend and soldier for the king; it was time to remind His Majesty of those facts while introducing his new bride.

"You've overlooked what I do believe is the best part," Emerlyn teased.

"And what, my love, is that?" He perked an eyebrow at her.

"True love's kiss," she whispered as her lashes fluttered at him.

Ever-so-slowly, he fused his warm lips to hers. Alaric felt a searing heat pulsate for just a moment as the tether between their two hearts weaved together into a golden glow. He nibbled her bottom lip, and Emerlyn dreamily sighed. Alaric had found his place in the world at long last, his home with his English lady. His adventures were only just beginning.

About: Michelle Helen Fritz

Michelle Helen Fritz was born in Maryland and raised in Arizona with lots of traveling throughout the States. She began her literary career as a personal assistant to Indie authors and loves to see the process of an idea turn into a finished book. Michelle loves to write about dashing heroes and the compelling women that tempt them with a dash of intrigue, an abundant amount of romance, and scenes that hopefully make her readers swoon. She is the mother of four children whom she homeschools and currently resides in Maryland with her own jaunty hero who makes all of her dreams come true.

You can follow Michelle on:

Amazon Author Page: Michelle Helen Fritz

Facebook: Author Michelle Helen Fritz

Instagram: Author Michelle Helen Fritz

Acknowledgements

This wouldn't be possible without my bestie, Ericka, who rescued me throughout this tale. This is just as much her story as it is mine. She is spectacular, and I promise to remind her of that when the world weighs her down.

Thank you to my Handsome Hubby as well as to my littles. You make every day an adventure.

Thank you so very much to Wanderlust Ink & Tomb L.L.C. for creating such a fabulous cover! I am tickled pink!

Brittany, the best PA ever: You rock. Thank you for all the things!

I have to mention Cathey again! Thank you so very much for all the polish you gave to this short story. It wouldn't be the same without your aid.

J.J. Marshall took this tale and made it flourish! Thank you so very much.

Lastly, thank you to YOU! You took a chance on my book and for that, I am forever grateful.

And thank you to my Creator. Every imagination needs some inspiration. Thank you for bestowing me with the gifts I have.

Also by: Michelle Helen Fritz

A Bramley Hall Regency Romance

Love At Last

Love That Lasts

Love Ever Lasting

Shades of Bramley Hall Regency Romance

Love Holds True

Courts & Curses

A Court Of Broken Dreams and Curse

A Court of Broken Promises and Nightmares

A Court of Broken Hopes and Wishes

Paullett Golden Anthology

Hourglass Romance: *Love At Rescue*

Romantic Choices: *Love Flames Anew*

Romantic Realms Anthology

Hearts At War: *Faerie Boots*

Shifting Hearts: *Faeriely Tart*

Beyond The Depths Anthology

A Bite of Winter & A Sip of Trouble: *Faerie Wishes*

www.ingramcontent.com/pod-product-compliance
Lightning Source LLC
Chambersburg PA
CBHW070550310726
48982CB00011B/1528/J

9798990381148